To Kayl
a love
hope

Best Regards,
Laura & Sergio
2/12/12

The ManWho Spoke With Cats

Written by T.E.Watson

Illustrated by Steve Ferchaud

 With Foreword by
The Clan Chattan USA

 HIGHLANDS CHILDREN'S PRESS

For Blue Eyes

Be happy my dear little one
For I'm not far away
Your Papa will be home soon
And again we both will play

T.E. Watson
©2006

The Man Who Spoke With Cats
Copyright ©2006 T.E. Watson

Published by Highlands Children's Press

Text/Story Copyright ©2004-2006 by T.E. Watson
Illustrations Copyright ©2006 Steve Ferchaud
Publisher; Heather and Highlands Press/Highlands Children's Press
Senior Editor; Rene' Schmidt

ISBN13 978-1-58478-019-9
ISBN 1-58478-019-3
EAN -9781584780199
Library of Congress Control Number (LCC) 2002093221

BISAC: JUV002050 Juvenile Fiction/Animals/Cats

Summary: This original Scottish folktale portrays the loyalty and friendship animals give freely to others.

Additional subjects: Pets, Folklore ,Country & Ethnic, Friendship.

Printed in Hong Kong First Edition First Printing 2006

Foreword

Scottish children's author, T. E. Watson, FSA Scot, has been a friend of Clan Chattan USA, the Clan Of The Cats, for many years. His children's stories, which are filled with insight into the world of the child as well as adults, are extraordinary.

His latest work, The Man Who Spoke With Cats, is an exceptional story. A Scottish folktale, it is heart warmingly conveyed with charm and elegance. It is a story to be shared with young and old alike. Cat owners around the world will instantly recognize elements of their own cats in this beautifully told tale. This book brings forth the importance of all our animal friends and how they enrich and touch our lives on a daily basis. Friendship, loyalty, dignity, companionship, and appreciation towards one another are values that this book extends to everyone.

Truly a gift, T.E. Watson communicates to the reader with style and charisma.

The Man Who Spoke With Cats will be a cherished addition to everyone's library and will take its place of honor in all Clan Chattan tents at all of the Highland Games we attend across the United States. We trust it will make its way into your heart and home.

Cindy Davis
Secretary and Treasurer
Clan Chattan USA

MacGregor sat in the porch swing enjoying the cool air of the new day. He watched his cats as they ate their morning meal, and as he sipped his tea he coaxed them with a pat of his knee.

One by one they jumped up. Little Face made herself at home in MacGregor's lap. Tavish and Cleo washed their paws and preened their ears, and Blue Eyes sat quietly next to MacGregor smiling contentedly into the warm rays of the sunrise.

"MacGregor, it's festival day. Are you going?" Tavish asked.

"Yes, are you? Will you bring a salmon or smoked herring from the mongers when you come home? Fresh fish tastes so delicious." Cleo said.

The old man stroked Little Face and said.

"I am going to visit friends. I will have my fill of bangers and mash, and then take a ride on the roundabout atop the tall white horse with the golden bridle. Come evening I will dance to music that makes my feet come alive, and at the end of the day I will watch the fireworks in all their colourful brilliance.

What will you do today?"

Little Face awoke with a contented yawning meow. She stretched from toes to tail, her claws gently piercing MacGregor's trousers.

"Well good morning girl. Are you ready for the day?" The old man asked.

"My day will be spent in the barley chasing midgies and hunting mice. I will be back this evening for supper."

She jumped down and headed for the fields.

Blue Eyes found a warm spot on the top table rock of the stone fence across the side yard. She stared for a time just looking off into the distance toward the village and soon she fell fast asleep.

Tavish went to lounge in the front yard underneath his favourite tree.

As for Cleo, she was happy to rest on the swing. MacGregor went off to the festival and left the cats to mind the house.

Morning lazily became noontime and as the sun reached mid-sky Tavish and Cleo met at the water dish.

"Bluc Eyes has gone off her perch. Have you seen her?" Cleo asked.

"She hasn't gone far, I'm sure." Tavish said.

Blue Eyes had not been herself for several days. Normally she was playful. She sniffed flowers and chased bugs. Her day was always filled with busy-ness. Of late she was always sleeping and not her lively self.

Cleo was concerned. Where has Blue Eyes gone? Perhaps she wants to find a new home. But what life could be better for a cat than to live here? Cleo did not understand.

Afternoon crawled by, and by supper time no sign of the Siamese. Another day passed and still no sign. Morning came and went for three more days. Blue Eyes had never been gone from home before. The gentle little cat had disappeared.

MacGregor was very worried.

He searched the village, and rustled through the barley, even through the bales. The more he searched the more worry set in. Where had this sweet feline gone?

He tried to keep his mind off Blue Eyes by tending his vegetable garden. Every so often he called out hoping she would hear and come scampering back home.

MacGregor again went into the village
to search. Cleo and Tavish went along and
helped look into every favourite napping spot
round the village.
No stone was left unturned.
But after a few hours, MacGregor
became tired and went back home.

Cleo continued searching for her friend. Tavish went home for an afternoon nap and when he arrived he found MacGregor sitting on the front steps gazing across the fields.

"Have you found any sign?" The old man asked sadly. "Not a whisker. My friend, she will be home soon. Try not to worry."

The kindly old man walked to
the stone fence and looked outward
toward the village.

"Where could she be?"

He sighed and went inside to rest in his favourite chair. He picked up the framed photo off the side table. It was the cats with him in the same chair during happier days, and before long he drifted off to sleep.

A new day's sun awoke the family. Cleo, Tavish, and Little Face were asleep on the blanket across his legs helping keep MacGregor warm.

When he served breakfast that morning it wasn't as enjoyable as usual. They all were still sad about Blue Eyes. She was not there to eat her favourite meal of salmon. MacGregor missed the little cat and blamed himself for her leaving. If he could only know she was doing well at her new home, it would ease his worry.

An early evening sunset found Tavish waiting at the edge of the porch. Little Face found the highest peak on the roof to span the best view of the village. Cleo sat herself on the porch rail gazing toward the stone fence.

Suddenly something made Cleo want to get closer for a better view. A faint light hearted meow was heard coming down the fence path in the distance.

All the cats perked up their ears with excitement. The meow was all too familiar.

Cleo called out.

"She's coming! Blue Eyes is coming home!"

The Siamese was skittering playfully about the top of the stone fence. She stopped to smell the jasmine and heather growing along side.

A moth flew out from the flowers and she tried to catch it.

Tavish leaped up on the railing and sat next to Cleo to see for himself. Little Face was close behind.

Blue Eyes was greeted with smiles and welcoming purrs.

"It's good to see you. Where have you have been?" Little Face asked.

"I will explain everything after dinner. Where is MacGregor? He must be sick with worry."

"He has been sad ever since you left. Your being home will brighten his mood." Tavish said.

The cats jumped from the fence and gathered round the food dish. They all meowed as loudly as their voices could.

"MacGregor, it's dinner time. Would you feed us please? Perhaps a bite of salmon would be good tonight." Cleo hinted.

"Hold on. I'll be there straight away." MacGregor said as he prepared the evenings supper.

The cats each sat at a corner of their dish. MacGregor opened the screen door and what he saw made his heartache disappear.

Smiling he asked. "When did you come home, little one?"

"I will tell you what I have been doing these last few days after dinner." Blue Eyes promised.

MacGregor reached down and gently petted her head.

"It is very good to see you, girl."

He went inside and sat in his chair very happy to know his family was together once more.

After dinner the cats went inside and settled in. Blue Eyes jumped up onto MacGregor's lap and took the seat of honour.
She turned in place to get comfortable, cleaned her whiskers, and then began to tell of her disappearance.

"MacGregor, many months ago you became sick with pneumonia. Do you remember how each of us stayed with you, taking care of you and keeping you from loneliness? I learned then I could keep others from their lonely times. That is what I have been doing."

"Yes, but where have you been and why so long? Is this why you have not been yourself?" Cleo asked.
"Yes, that is why I was not as playful as you are used to. I was tired and worried about a friend." Blue Eyes continued.

"Mrs. Fraser, who lives in the village became ill. Her heart was weak and she had no one to care for her.
That is why I have been so tired. I helped her every day. I slept in her lap, brought a mouse as a gift, and watched her smile as we chatted.

I stayed with her for these days because she needed me. I came home today because my help was no longer needed. She was not lonely anymore. Mrs. Fraser passed away peacefully last night while she slept."

A quiet silence came over the family. MacGregor smiled with pride as a tear rolled down his cheek as he reflected on the great kindness Blue Eyes had given.

"I left her resting. The village is honouring her tomorrow afternoon. She was a bonny old woman." Blue Eyes finished.

Cleo jumped up next to Blue Eyes and placed a paw on one of hers.

"You gave her last minutes dignity as well, my friend. We will all honour Mrs. Fraser as you have honoured us."

Cleo licked Blue Eye's nose and curled up next to her.

The evening's hours ticked calmly by. The family was together and all worries were gone. MacGregor sat quietly with the cats in his comfy chair looking out the front window watching the stars.

The cats settled in for the night, with Blue Eyes purring in MacGregor's lap.

And they awoke together in the morning, as was their way.

Glossary of Scottish Words in this Book

Bangers -A type of sausage from Scotland. During the Second World War, sausages contained so much water they exploded, when fried, with a bang.

Barley -A major food and animal feed crop, and is a member of the grass family.

Heather -A flower with a rich purple glow. It fills the Scottish hillsides with vast colour and has become a well-loved national symbol.

Jasmine -An old world climbing plant or shrub that bares fragrant flowers that are used in perfumes and teas.

Mash -In Scotland and throughout the United Kingdom the word mash is short for a special recipe of mashed potato.

Midgies -Scotland's type of large mosquito.

Monger -A dealer or trader in a specified product such as a Fishmonger or Cheese monger.

Roundabout -The United Kingdom's word for a merry-go-round. It is also known as a turning circle for automobiles.

Smoked Herring -A type of ocean fish. A dried and smoked herring has a reddish colour. It is considered a great meal for both humans and cats, and is a delicious addition for breakfast in Scotland.

Table Rock -The cap stone or top stone for a stone fence. It helps to level out the sight line for the fence and makes a great place to sit or rest.

Award Wining Children's Author T.E. Watson
and his wonderful cat/agent Ceilidh.
Pronounced Kaylee, the name means *celebration*
in Scots Gaelic.

T.E. Watson is the author of over 92 stories
for children.

His two latest are *The Man Who Spoke
With Cats*, and the long awaited *Glen
Robbie, A Scottish Fairy Tale*.

His books include the award winning
I Wanna Iguana, *The Monster In The
Mailbox*, and *Mom Can I Have A Dragon?*.

T.E. Watson is available for speaking
engagements, and school visits.

You can see his web site at
www.tewatsononline.com.
You may contact T.E.Watson via e-mail at
tew@tewatsononline.com.

Steve Ferchaud is an internationally known
artist and illustrator. He has over a dozen children's
books to his credit including another of T.E. Watson's
entitled Glen Robbie A Scottish Fairy Tale. ISBN 978-1-58478-014-4
He has also written and illustrated three of his own creation;
Gnome Poems, Ace Banndage, and The Leaf Painter.
You can visit his web site at www.steveferchaud.com.